you belong here

Written by M.H. Clark

Illustrated by Isabelle Arsenault

The stars belong in the deep night sky
and the moon belongs there too,
and the winds belong in each place they blow by

and I
belong here
with you.

The whales and the fishes belong in the sea
and the waves belong by the shore,
and the dune's where the grasses belong to be
because grasses are what dunes are for.

And the trees belong in the wild wood
and the deer belong in their shade,

and the birds belong so safe and good
and warm in the nests that they've made.

And you belong where you love to be,
and after each day is through,
you will always belong right next to me
and I'll belong next to you.

The frogs and the lilies belong in the lake,
where the water is silver and clear,

and the turtles belong in the homes that they make
in the sand where the water is near.

And the otters belong by the banks of the stream
and the cattails belong there too,

and the carp belong where the water runs green
and the shadows all run blue.

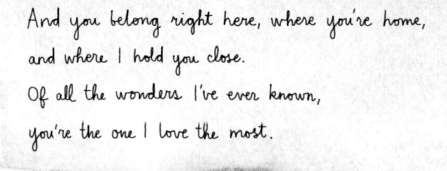

And you belong right here, where you're home,
and where I hold you close.
Of all the wonders I've ever known,
you're the one I love the most.

The hares belong in the desert air
where the rocks are red and gold,
and those rocks belong with the comets out there,
which flash bright when the night turns cold.

The foxes belong in the high canyon hills
and the sage there belongs in the sun,

and the lizards belong in the light, sitting still,
until they are ready to run.

The crickets belong in the old stone wall
and the bees belong in the clover,

just as winter belongs in its place after fall,
before the new year starts over.

And you are a dream that the world once dreamt
and now you are part of its song.
That's why you are here, in the place where you're meant,
for this is right where you belong.

The pines belong on the mountainsides,
tucked under their blankets of snow,
and the bears belong in the caves where they hide
whenever the storms start to blow.

Some creatures were made for the land, or the air,
and others were made for the sea;
each creature is perfectly home right there
in the place it belongs to be.

And no matter what places you travel to,
what wonders you choose to see,
I will always belong right here with you,
and you'll always belong with me.

M.H. Clark

M.H. Clark is a poet and writer who has received
multiple awards including the Washington State Book
Award and two Moonbeam Children's Book Awards.
She has traveled the world and lived in many wonderful
places—but she believes she belongs most of all in
a tiny house with a large library, someplace where the
forest meets the sea.

Isabelle
Arsenault

Isabelle Arsenault is an award-winning illustrator,
whose work has received international recognition and
multiple honors, including three prestigious Governor
General Awards for Children's Literature and two
nominations for the New York Times Best Illustrated
Children's Books. She draws her inspiration from
all kinds of places and eras, but feels most at home in
Montreal surrounded by the family and artists she loves.

WITH SPECIAL THANKS TO THE ENTIRE
COMPENDIUM FAMILY.

Credits:
Written by: M.H. Clark
Illustrated by: Isabelle Arsenault
Edited by: Amelia Riedler and Kristin Eade
Art Direction by: Heidi Dyer and Jill Labieniec

Library of Congress Control Number: 2015955980
ISBN: 978-1-938298-99-8

3rd printing. Printed in China with soy inks. A051709003